Killer Truck

About Story and Author

Author Thapandas E Menon is one with social views and responsibilities. As we all know NCB and Indian Navy caught 2500kg drugs, worth 15000 crores from a boat in Indian waters, near Kochi, on May 2023 and the mother ship was sunk. This event exposed the serious threat of chemical drugs coming to our country. We all know these chemical drugs like MDMA, Meth, Molly, Shabu, etc. are now circulating among our Indian youth. Now these drugs are unavoidable in new generation parties. Many greedy criminals are coming forward for this business because of large profit incorporated. Drugs are coming from Afghanistan, Iran and Pakistan which is delivered in motherships. They are collected in boats and unloaded at Indian ports. Our villain in this story is also a criminal came into drug business for profit. Please enjoy reading, how our hero adventurously and courageously challenged the villain and busted him in the end.

Disclaimer

In America, officials retired from government agencies like Army, CIA, FBI, DEA are many times spotted as criminals, drug lords, smugglers and illegal weapons dealers. Using the training and skills, they got from American agencies they are committing crimes for profit. These are quoted in many movies, many times. Motivated from the story of these American corrupt officials, our author Thapandas E Menon wrote this story with small changes made. For making the story suitable for Indian readers some changes are made like American army is changed to Indian army in the story. American soldier is changed to Indian soldier. American government agencies are changed to Indian government agencies. Instead of America, some real events and paper cuttings are quoted from India. But everything is just fiction and imagination, made only for entertainment.

This is a work of fiction. Names, character, business, events and incidents are the products of the author's imagination. Any resemblance to actual persons, living or dead, or actual events is purely coincidental. This story and characters are fictitious. Certain long-standing institutions, agencies, and public offices are mentioned. But the characters involved are wholly imaginary. The role played by Colonel Norbert in this story is entirely fictional. This story and characters have no factual basis.

Author Thapandas E Menon is proud to be an Indian. He has great respect and love towards Indian army and Indian soldiers. Indian army and Indian soldiers are equivalent to gods, who protects and guards our country and its borders in extreme weather conditions. Their sacrifice, determination, honesty and love for their country can never be questioned. This story is purely fictitious and no factual connection with Indian army or Indian soldiers and other government agencies.

Copyright

Table of content

Colonel Norbert

Army people are always respected in our country for their bravery, honesty, sacrifice and hardship at work. They are dedicated and uncorrupted. But everything has an analogy or a black mark. Colonel Norbert is such a black mark in army. He is corrupted, drunkard and womanizer. He will do anything for money. Army officials took many disciplinary actions against him, none of these changed him. He only developed his knowledge to do the corruption much better next time without getting caught. He is a handsome man of age forty. His wife and children left him because of these bad habits. His only companion in the world is two like-minded corrupted subordinates.

As the article 370 was revoked by India government, the special status of Jammu Kashmir was cancelled. Thus Indian army got endless power in Kashmir Valley. Terrorists are nearly neutralized. Their weapons are seized and camps are demolished. But Pakistan army, Pakistan terrorists and ISI are still trying to supply weapons and money to Kashmir militants. Still many people from other states of India working in Kashmir are getting killed by terrorists. Weapons are smuggling to India across border by drone and other means. These smuggled weapons are distributed to terrorists by some criminals in Kashmir, by taking money. Colonel Norbert has good relationship with these criminals and gets bribery for helping them distribute the smuggled weapons and drugs. Colonel patrol in army jeep with his two like-minded and corrupted subordinates. They stop at check post and act like helping the guards. While the smuggling vehicle comes, Colonel and his men comes forward and inspects it and ensures its safe passage. This is done in various check posts. These smugglings in Kashmir valley are mainly conducted by a criminal leader named Rana. Rana has a luxury hotel in Kashmir valley. For tourists, lots of night party, drugs, prostitution and various illegal activities are conducted there. By taking bribe Colonel and his two subordinates gives full support to Rana. Rana will get information hours before any raid occur in hotel, so he never gets caught. Besides bribe, Colonel and his men gets food, drink, drugs, women and everything for free in Rana's camp.

Once Colonel Norbert was so drunk that he fell on road. Local police arrested him without knowing he was a Colonel and filed a FIR against him. Next day when he got out, he and his two subordinates came back to police station with gun and threatened the police. They fired at glasses and walls of police station. Since, if this incident is known to outside world, it will be a shame for both army and police. So senior officials of both departments made a compromise. Colonel and his subordinates were warned by senior officials and got punished.

Colonel Norbert's life became hell after this incident. Every other family in other army quarters kept Colonel away, because he is a womanizer. Major Ram Lal was also not in touch with Colonel. Ram Lal has a beautiful wife and two daughters. Elder daughter Nandini was as beautiful as his mother. She was doing degree in army college. Colonel had an eye on her. Ram Lal had a drinking problem. Knowing this once Colonel invited Ram Lal to his quarters for drinking. Ram Lal started to give company to Colonel for drinking in Colonel's quarters and they became friends. Once Colonel said there is no one here to cook some side dish for drinking, can we go to your quarters, so that your wife could cook us some side dish. Ram Lal took Colonel home and from that day they started to gather in Ram Lal's quarters. When seeing outside, Colonel started little chats with Nandini. She didn't feel anything wrong in talking with father's friend. Nandini fell in love with Colonel, they started making out while gets a chance. One day Nandini took Colonel to Ram Lal and said I am in love with Colonel and wish to marry him. Ram Lal lost temper, he took his service pistol and try to shoot Colonel. Ram Lal's wife and Nandini stopped him from firing the gun. Seeing this Colonel ran away from the scene. Ram Lal was crying and don't know what to do. At this time Nandini said "Please don't separate us now daddy, I am pregnant". Ram Lal was fed up. Next day his wife found him dead. His dead body was hanging from the fan in dining room. He wrote a suicide note saying "how will I face my coworkers, friends and relatives. I don't want to live with the burden of such a shame". After Ram Lal's death, his family hasn't filed any compliant against Colonel, thinking about the future of Nandini, She took an abortion and the family went back to their native state. Everyone in army base become agitated and tensed knowing the reason of Ram Lal's death. Everyone in that base, including other officers and the head of base Brigadier General started punishing, harassing and torturing colonel, whenever they got a chance. If nothing comes up, they will make something for harassing colonel. Colonel thought Pakistan jail would be better than this.

Knowing Colonel's condition Rana put forward an offer. India has bought S-400 Triumph system from Russia. It is a surface-to-air missile (SAM) system. India has already deployed its first squadron of S- 400 at north in Punjab. S-400 is composed of several units, one of which is radar system unit. This radar system unit has very much demand in international weapons black market. But this S- 400 system is heavily guarded by Indian military by a special security battalion. They will guard 24 hours. Rana said with his political influence, he will arrange deputation for Colonel and his two subordinates, to the security battalion of S-400. Colonel has to blow a fire cracker at a corner to create a deviation. Then everyone will gather around there. At that time, a truck full of Rana's men will enter there with machine guns and grenades and start a surprise attack. They will steel the military truck containing radar unit of s 400 and flee the scene. A squadron of S-400 costs nearly 1650 crore and this radar system unit alone will cost 500 crores. Rana will give 100 crores to colonel in Singapore bank and a fake Singapore passport for staying in Singapore. According to colonel that was jackpot and a life time settlement. He felt that offer just like a dope.

Colonel and two subordinates are deputed to security battalion of S-400. The day of action had come, Colonel was told to use fire cracker at 10.00 am. Rana's men will enter after a minute. But unexpected happened, central intelligence has got information about this plot. Central agency RAW caught one of Rana's men and military raided Rana's camp. They killed Rana and his men, unfortunately nobody was alive to tell anything about Colonel's hand in this plot. At 9.45 am, five trucks of army entered the compound with enough soldiers to fight a small war. Senior officials told Colonel that they got information about an attack on S-400 system. Since all senior officials are nearby Colonel was unable use fire cracker. Rana's men who were staying in nearby house, without knowing Rana's death and failure of plot, entered the compound in a truck like a mouse getting into the trap and a huge fire fight occurred. Army got only small casualties and all the Rana's remaining men were dead. During this fight Colonel killed his two subordinates and told everyone, they got killed in the attack. Colonel knows Rana and his men are dead, now only one knows Colonel's link with this attack is his subordinates. Colonel don't have to think twice for a couple of homicide, even if that was his beloved buddies.

Colonel Norbert

Pakistan smuggling weapons across the border by drones, caught by army

India's S -400 Triumph System bought from Russia

After this incident army started a through enquiry but no one had any clue about Colonel's involvement in this incident. But all the officers in the security battalion of S-400 at the time of attack were under suspicion and all of them got transferred and relieved from major responsibilities. Colonel was transferred to Himachal base camp

Colonel was a black sheep in the Himachal army camp also. Other officers kept him away from him and the Brigadier General who was the head of that camp also disliked him and avoided him from major responsibilities. Himachal base camp was a hell to Colonel. Without bribery, parties and women, he was getting exhausted. Then he started to find new ways of corruption. Colonel was given the charge of store and ration supply of camp. Its Colonels responsibility to give the ration which includes liquor, boots, sweater, gloves and other accessories. He takes all these things from store and sells in black market. And after that this will be shown as ration given to low rank officers. They are afraid to raise voice against Colonel so kept silent. The liquor bottles are delivered to camp store from warehouse, in carton boxes (cardboard boxes). There will be 20 bottles in one carton box. Colonel hits this carton box with stick and breaks the bottle inside this carton box without opening the seal of carton box. The liquor will come out through small air holes in the bottom of the carton boxes. This liquor is collected, filtered and transferred to new bottles and sold in black market. Since the seal of the carton box is not opened, it is entered as defected during transportation in register book and send backs to warehouse. Nearly 15 to 20 such carton boxes are sent back to warehouse as defected during loading and transportation, every month. But as time passes, higher rank officers including Brigadier General starts to doubt Colonel. Now Colonel really is tensed, because if low rank officers tell the truth to Brigadier General, Colonel will have to go to jail. Colonel is now thinking to get out of army and start some new business.

Once colonel and some assistants went to market in uniform for purchasing accessories for army camp store. When others were doing purchase, Colonel went outside to drink a cup of tea. While sitting and enjoying the tea in a tea shop, Colonel saw a young man named Joyal stealing a purse from someone's pocket. He took the purse and started walking, but suddenly he saw Colonel in uniform, staring at him. Joyal was feared and stood frozen. Joyal put the purse down and walked out of the tea shop. Colonel caught him outside the tea shop. Colonel scolded and threatened him just like a cat playing with a mouse. The young man said his name is Joyal and was a driver, but lost his job. Now starving to eat something, that's why he did it. Joyal begged Colonel that "please don't arrest him, he will do anything". As we say like minds attracts each other. Colonel liked him and told him to come with colonel, as his driver.

Himachal Base Camp

Drug smuggling boat caught in Indian waters by Indian Navy

At this time an incident happened, which was a turning point in Colonel's life. NCB and Army along with navy conducted a covert operation in Arabian sea against drugs. Large shipment of drugs coming to Arabian sea from Afghanistan in mother ships, which will then be transferred to Indian ports in small boats and then distributed to major cities of India. Army sent the officers from Himachal camp for this operation. Army and Navy surrounded one of the drug peddlers boat filled with drugs like MDMA, meth, heroin, etc. There was a huge exchange of fire between both sides. All the drug peddlers got killed, except one who was wounded. He was a Pakistan citizen named Zameer Ali and was taken to military hospital near Himachal base camp for treatment and further interrogations. All the officers in Himachal camp were busy sorting and filing the captured drugs, for reporting to the higher authorities. So Colonel was given the security charge of Zameer Ali in the hospital.

When in hospital Zameer got a chance to chat with Colonel. Zameer came to know Colonel was corrupted. Zameer offered him a good business deal. Afghanistan mountains are famous for poppy plants, which used to make drugs. He will deliver drugs in Arabian sea or Bengal sea in ships. Colonel can become the distributor of cities like Bangalore, Chennai and Kochi and control the south Indian belt of Zameer's boss's business. Zameer told him drugs like MDMA and meth can be sold hundred times the original value in cities. Colonel understood it was his chance. He helped Zameer to escape from the hospital and marked dead in hospital and military records. As Zameer reached Pakistan, he contacted colonel and discussed about the plan of action.

Colonel took voluntary retirement from army and bought a bungalow in the hill town of Anandpur, which is in south India and nearer to sea, where ships can be sailed much closer to land. Colonel wanted some quite place and avoid suspicions. Anandpur town is at the top of Sreenidhi mountain and only one road way up. People there are illiterate and mostly cattle farmers. Colonel asked his driver Joyal to join him, so that he will give a good share of business. Thus both went to Anandpur and started drug business. Colonel hired lots of hatchet man to do his smuggling and dirty works. Drugs from Afghanistan are delivered at sea in mother ships. Colonel sends boat to collect these drugs and then distributed to drug dealers in major cities for further supply. Colonel started to get large profit from drug smuggling. Colonel maintained a good image before society of Anandpur. For showing others he ran many businesses like large cattle farm, liquor factory and distillery, etc. Everything is to hide his drug business from outside world. He kept his drug business real secret.

Sreenidhi Mountains

Akshay took charge

Two years later, another place, another time.

Office of Hindustan Current News Channel in Bengaluru is busy with Election news and hot political discussions. Elections are nearby, predictions like exit polls are dancing on news channel screens. Even in this hurry burry, routine works are also going well on other side. Chief Editor Joseph Mathan called for senior sub editor Akshay. Akshay entered editor's cabin and took his seat. Mathan started explaining about Akshay's new assignment. Akshay got embarrassed hearing his senior, with a nervous facial expression he asked

Akshay : "Are you out of your mind, you want such a senior staff like me to make a report on some silly cattle breed. I mean, many other news channels are ready to give me anything for a journal of mine. This type of works are supposed to be done by some junior staff. I am a detective journalist who busted four corrupt government officials, two politicians and lastly a land mafia. I risked my life in this I am threated from four sides of society."

Mathan : "Don't get upset and agitated. I am not trying to insult you by giving this. This is not what you think. Vechur cow is a rare breed with a height of two and a half feet. It is the world's smallest cattle breed. It produces larger amount of milk with large protein content and medicinal value. But it is now in critical maintained breed list. Government has come up with new program for increasing its numbers and dairy farm income of the state. It is also their political strategy for upcoming elections. Every news channel has their own political interest. Minister's personal assistant directly called me and requested for boosting this news. If I give this assignment to some junior staff, they will give me some low quality content, I don't want that. I just wanted a detailed and studied report, and that's why I choose you. Also you are having threats from land mafia, it will be good, if you leave the city for some time, until the scene cools off. Anandpur mountain town is famous for vechur cattle farms. I have already arranged a house there for you. You just stay there for three months and give me a detailed report."

Akshay was not pleased with his editor. But corporate world is like that, sometimes you have to work against your will and emotions. Without saying a word Akshay took the files and details and left the cabin.

Akshay got back to his seat and was upset and sitting lazy. His colleague, Daisy saw him and had a smile. They discussed about his new assignment. Daisy was his good friend and had small crush on him. Hearing everything Daisy said

Daisy : "Let's leave the office early and go out for a shopping. We can purchase the needy things for your journey and see some movie together."

Hearing Daisy's words, Akshay really felt like a rain in desert. He decided to go on with Daisy's plan.

They left the office and purchased necessary things. After a movie they just went to a nice hotel for dinner. Both of them went to Akshay's place for making out. At last Akshay dropped Daisy to her home and returned to his flat. Akshay thought it was really a battery charging and every one must have such a girlfriend in life. Akshay was ready to take the new challenge by hearing Daisy's motivational words. He started to gear up his mind for this journey.

Akshay

Early morning Akshay started the journey to Anandpur town, in the top of Sreenidhi mountain in his own car. Akshay loves self driving and long trips. He started to drive the car and enjoyed the road trip. He sometimes stopped on road sides for refreshment. His back started to ache due to hours of sitting in the car and driving. But none of these can spoil his spirit and Akshay continued his trip. Car reached the bottom of the Sreenidhi mountain, there was a check post and two guards. Guard's checked the papers and car started to climb the mountain. While going up the mountain, he saw a boy selling oranges on road side. He was not in need of fruits at that time, but seeing that innocent boy, he decided to buy some oranges. Boy sold some oranges to Akshay and gave him an advice

Boy: "Please be careful, there is a sharp hairpin bend road coming ahead. Lots of accidents happens there."

Akshay just smiled and continued driving.

After half an hour, as the boy said, came a deep hairpin bend road. Car passed that hair pin climb and moved forward.

Akshay drove the car for sometimes and stopped the car, when he saw a good scenery. With his dslr camera he clicked some snaps. He walked near a valley and washed his face and it really was like heaven. He roamed on the mountain with camera, clicking stills.

After some walk, he saw a plane land. There was a helicopter parked and two people were doing some repair on it. Akshay thought it was some sight-seeing helicopter. It will be good if he can take some pictures from the sky. With happiness he just shouted from a distance

Akshay : "Hey guys , can I have minute. "

They saw Akshy walking towards them. At this time, one of the men took out a pistol from his pocket and started to fire towards Akshay. Akshay ran like hell, holding his life in his hand. He took shelter behind a tree. The two men suddenly flee the scene with helicopter. Akshay don't understand anything, is it a nightmare, he can't believe all these happened were real. He stood behind that tree, shocked for ten minutes. After that he slowly came out and walked to the position where helicopter was parked. There were some fluid on the ground, it was oil or fuel. Akshy thought they were pouring some fuel or oil into the engine. Akshay saw a cover above the rock nearby. In the hurry burry of fleeing, they forgot to take the cover. Akshay took the cover and checked inside. There was a map of the mountain, on the map there were three points, it was joined in such a way that, a V-shape is created. Akshay thought they will be doing some illegal activities like killing rhinos or elephants for tusk. They might thought Akshay as a police men looking for them. That might be the reason for shooting.

Akshay got back to his car and started driving. After half an hour, reached the Anandpur mountain town. At the entrance of the town there was another check post. While guards checking the car, Akshay step outside and there was a hotel nearby. Aksahy ordered a coffee and enjoyed sipping it slowly. It was lunch time and hotel owner was not impressed with Akshay. Akshay decided not to talk anything about helicopter and shooting. He enquired more about the town and cattle farms to the lady supplier who was a kind person.

Akshay continued his journey and with the help of google map, found out the house arranged by Mathen. Akshay unpacked his luggage and get settled in the house. There was a watchman in that house, who showed him the house. Sherly and Edwin were neighbours living in nearby house. Sharly came to Akshay and introduced herself. Sherly told Akshay that Mathan had made the food arrangements of Akshay, in Sharleys house. She will be delivering the food for him. She gave some food and refreshments to Akshay. Akshay started to plan his work and schedule. At night Akshay went to Sherly's house for dinner. After dinner they had a little chat. Sherly introduced her husband, Edwin. Akshay explained about his job and his intentions in Anandpur town. Edwin offered his full cooperation, since Akshay is a new bee to town. Akshay went home and had a good sleep. His mobile alarm rang at morning 6.00 am. Akshay took the whiskey bottle and fixed a peg to relieve from yesterday's hangover. He geared up for his routine morning walk, and is not ready to avoid it even if he is away from home.

After sometime, sun rises and light rays hit the mountain. Roads are clear and Akshay got back home. After taking a bath and completing his usual routines, he went to neighbour Sherly's house for breakfast. Akshay asked about cattle farm locations in Anandpur town. Sherly told Edwin to accompany Askay to cattle farms. Akshay and Edwin visited some cattle farms that day. Aksay thought it is not fair to bother others for his work. Next day he decided to go alone with the help of google map, driving his own car. For refilling the car, Akshay drove to fuel pump down the mountain. He went to a tea shop nearby. People there was sharing some gossips and local politics. In the middle of these talks, someone started the discussion about the danger hairpin road and the suspicious accidents happened there. Akshay also heard someone saying about a ghost truck making these accidents. Akshay smiled inside and thought people are still believing these ghost stories in this 21st century.

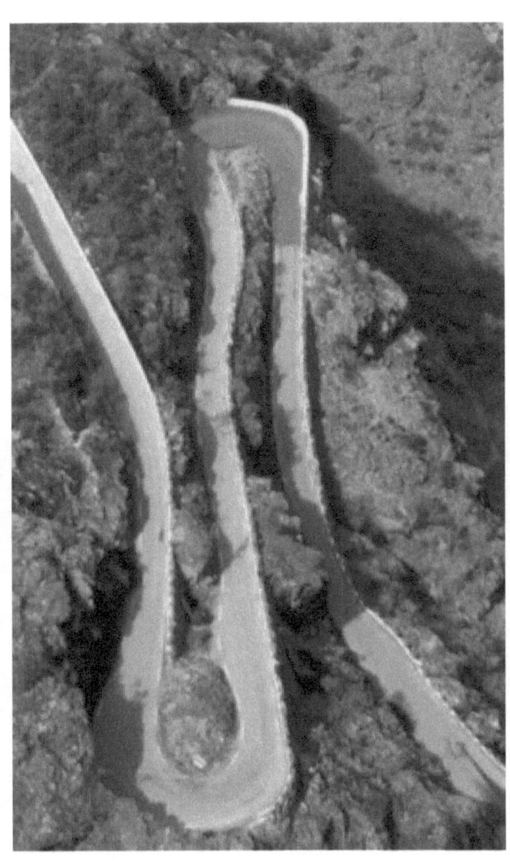

Danger Hairpin Bend Road

Veterinary Doctor

Akshay went roaming in Anandpur town in his car. He visited many cattle farms and collected the details. Farmers were cooperative and friendly. while visiting a farm, Hearing the loud noise of helicopter, Akshay asked the farm owner

Akshay : "Whose is this helicopter, what's its purpose in this mountain".

Farm owner : "no one knows that, where is it coming from and going to. Many people tried to find it out,but not yet found. Veterinary doctor David is the one who hates this vehicle most. According to him, this loud noise of helicopter will terrify the cattle and will reduce the amount of milk produced. Doctor David kept enquiring to find the owner of this helicopter. I don't know if he found that."

Akshay : "Where can I find this doctor."

Farm owner : "His house is down the mountain. But he is working in a veterinary hospital in Anandpur town. It will be working during the day time. You can go and see him there."

Akshay visited two or more farms and got back home. He discussed about this doctor to his neighbour and Sherly's husband, Edwin. Edwin said that this doctor is an expert in cattle caring. He is the only veterinary doctor in the mountain. He visits the cattle farms regularly and take care of cattle. Farm owners love him and gives him dairy products as gifts besides his fees. I know him personally and is a good friend of mine. I will take you to his dispensary, tomorrow itself.

Next day Akshy and Edwin went to Doctor's dispensary. Edwin took Akshay to doctor's room, but no one was there. Edwin asked the staff about the doctor. Staff was sad and explained doctor David had an accident last night at the danger hairpin road. David is admitted in the hospital's Intensive care unit, down the mountain.

Edwin and Akshay heisted to hospital and enquired about David at the reception. They stood before ICU and waited for the specialist doctor to come. Specialist doctor came out of ICU and said that Davis's condition is severe, and can't let them see David. Edwin said they were good friends, please give him a minute. Specialist doctor said "be quick and don't disturb him".

Edwin along with Akshay entered ICU and saw David in bed. Edwin asked David, how this happened. David slowly explained "It was a truck which caused this accident. When I reached the danger hair pin a truck suddenly hit on the back of my car. I was sure there were no truck behind my car till I reached the danger hair pin. I don't know where did it suddenly came from. I don't know why my cars airbag system didn't work. That truck dragged my car to the edge of mountain and throw it off the mountain. My head hit somewhere hard and I lost my consciousness. I saw the truck only once but I am sure it was Jeromes's truck. When I got consciousness, I am in hospital. They told me they got me from a half-destroyed car, from the bottom of mountain trench."

Akshay and Edwin got out of ICU and discussed about the accident. Edwin said

Edwin : "Only a few survived these accidents . All of them told the same story of this truck. Same Jerome's truck. I can understand other illiterate people explaining about ghost truck. But I am not able to digest when, Dr.David, a person who is related to science explains about a ghost truck."

Akshay : "Didn't you hear what he said . David's head was hit hard on something while accident, I think David has not regained his mental health completely. I think When he gets out of this shock, he will change his story. First let's wait and pray for him to survive this accident."

About Anandpur and danger hairpin bend road

While taking dinner at Sherly house, that night, Akshay discussed about the gossips he overheard about the danger hairpin road. According to Edwin, danger hairpin road is a curse of this mountain. Many says there is a ghost, some says it's because of careless driving, some other scientific guys says the magnetic attraction of earth is more in that place and cars are attracted, some says its due to unscientific construction of that road, no one knows the exact truth.

Edwin continued, Anandpur town is situated at the top of Srinidhi mountain nearer to sea in south India with a population of about fifty thousand people. There is only one road way up from bottom of the mountain to its top. There is a check post at the bottom of the mountain and another check post at the top, where the Anandpur town starts. In Between these two check posts there is no house, shop or any other building, only plane mountain and grass lands. At the middle of these check posts there lies the danger hairpin bend road. Danger hairpin road is a sharp U-shaped hairpin bend road, with one side mountain rocks and other side deep mountain trench. At this Danger hairpin many accidents happened and lots of vehicle fell off the mountain. Accidents are a usual thing in this turn. Another mystery about these accidents was the airbags were not working during accidents, in these cars. This really increased the chance of victim's death. Many gossips and rumors are spreading about this danger hairpin. There was a truck driver named Jerome lived in Anandpur town. Once he along with his truck vanished at this danger hairpin. People are saying it's his ghost making these accidents. Very few people survived these accidents, what they explained were shocking. A truck hit on the back of their car and the description of the truck given by them exactly matches the Jerome's truck. Another mysterious fact is that on the day of these accidents there was no truck passed through both up and down check posts. Between these two check posts there is no place to hide a truck because there is only grass land and plane mountain. Not even a cycle can be parked without anyone seeing. Police patrol all over the mountain but unable to find such truck. As the first step of investigation, police fixed CCTV camera's and hidden camera's at this danger turn covering different angles. Accidents also took place after this, but every camera's electronic board were destroyed just hours before the accidents using electromagnetic pulse waves. No one knows who produced such waves, from where, or if such waves are produced by nature itself during some cosmic activities. Electronic devices including mobile phones in a three kilometer radius are destroyed while this electromagnetic pulse wave bursts. when these electromagnetic pulse wave comes, electronic circuits get overloaded which destroys the electronic devices completely. As next step police posted a constable named Raman to guard this danger hairpin, one day, he suddenly vanished during his duty time at danger hairpin. Constable Raman was missing from that day, no one ever heard anything about him, after that. Then another two police constables also got missing in same manner while in guard duty at danger hairpin. After that, no police men ever shown courage to take duty at danger hairpin. As these set of incidents occurred, People in Anandpur town are really feared and life threatened. They don't know what to do, even police force abandoned them. Night travelling is nearly avoided by people and they are very careful in passing this turn now.

Jerome's Truck

Akshay: "For whom Jerome was working , during his last days."

Edwin: "There is a Colonel living up the mountain. He is the richest man in Anandpur. He has lots of business. Colonel has a liquor factory and distillery. Jerome used to work for Colonel by transporting his cargos and goods. Jerome got missing while working for this Colonel. But Colonel says he don't know anything about this man missing. Police enquired this case but found no clues. This Colonel has got a cattle farm which is the biggest one in Anandpur. Haven't you visited there yet."

Akshay: "no, not yet, May I know where this farm is."

Aksahy got the location of farm from Edwin. Next day he drove to Colonel's farm and meet the farm manager. Farm manager showed him the farm and explained about cattle breeds and caring them. They showed the verity of dairy products, produced by that farm. During the time of leave, Aksahy asked manager about the owner. Askay said he is interested to meet the owner of such a huge and nice farm.

Farm manger took him to Colonel's house and introduced him to Colonel and left the house. Colonel invited Aksahy inside for a cup of tea. Aksahy and Colonel were enjoying the tea in the garden at the backyard of Colonel's house. Colonel told many things about farm, dairy products and his other businesses like liquor and distillery. In the middle of this discussion Akshay asked about Jerome's case. Colonel said police and town people asked me the same question, but what I say, unfortunately I don't know anything, he has got missing one day, that's what I know."

While they were talking a servant came and said someone called colonel on land phone, he must attend the call, its urgent. Colonel asked Akshay to enjoy the tea and he will be back in a minute. Aksahy just stood up and walked around watching the beauty of Colonel's backyard garden. Suddenly Akshay noticed a cable going from the house to backyard. He just followed the cable. The cable was mounted to a tree, at the end of the cable there is a red beacon light. This light was fixed on the tree in upward direction. Akshay also found two other such red lights on two other separate trees. He didn't understand anything. He was standing below the light thinking. Then he got back to his chair and start sipping the tea. Colonel got back after some time. Akshay acted like nothing happened and asked nothing about the cables and light. They continued their chat.

Akshay went home and was confused about this upward pointed beacon lights seen on the garden. He searched on internet for answers. Findings were little breath taking. According to google, such upward directed red beacon lights are normally used in Aviation industry, in order to signal a plane or helicopter for dropping a package from the air without landing the plane or helicopter. Using red beacon lights they will make shapes of alphabets like H,L,T,N,V,etc and plane can see this from large distance during night. Thus the plane can come and go after dropping the package on the spot, without landing.

Akshay just remembered the helicopter shooting incident. He got a cover containing a map, with three points connected to form a V-shape, from the rock on the day of helicopter shooting incident. The three red beacon lights in Colonel's backyard will form a V-shape. So the helicopter had come to drop something on Colonel's backyard. Now Akshay got clear view about the owner of the helicopter he saw. Colonel got liquor factory and distillery. Helicopter might be dropping the black money for an exchange spirit barrels in black market. He decided there is much to do in Anandpur, besides just a cattle farm documentary. Akshay decided to enquire more about Colonel and his business.

Snack delivery

Sherly makes and delivers home made cakes, pastries and snacks to neighborhood. Sherly also delivers to Colonel's house. Colonel conducts various business meets in the conference room of his house. Sherly delivers snacks and refreshments for a small cost. She had access to Colonel's house and office room attached to it. Knowing this, Akshay decided to seek for Sherly's help. Akshay shared his interests to Sherly and said he wanted to clear his suspicions. Akshay offered descent price for spying on Colonel. Sherly was impressed and was ready to do what he says. Akshay told her, while meeting takes place on conference room, nobody will be there on nearby office room. So after the delivery of snacks to conference room, just enter office room without anyone seeing. Just take photos of documents and files above the table. Repeat this process every time you get a chance.

As Akshay said, Sherly started to spy on Colonel for money. She gave the pictures of lots of files. Some of the pictures really pointed out

Colonel's illegal activities. As per Akshay said, Sherly stole such files and documents. This process went for some time, until that day, one of the Colonel's men saw Sherly in office room taking some files. Sherly just got panic, put the files back on shelf. She just smiled and said I heard some noise from the office room, I was checking if it was some mouse or something. Sherly's reply was not completely digested by Colonel's men, but he just stood still at that time. Sherly just walked away like nothing happened. Colonel's men informed everything to Colonel, he was angry and his facial expression showed the keen decision he took on his mind.

Sherly reached home and was shivering with fear. She went to Akshay and told everything happed, she said they are bad and will do anything. Akshay told her to calm down, nothing will happen. He reassured, there is police and law and no one will harm you. you are just like my sister and I will definitely protect you. Hearing this Sherly went home and relaxed.

After an hour a car came in front of Sherly's house. Five men entered Sherly house and one of them asked her to take all the documents she took from Colonel's office. He had a gun pointed to Sherly. She gave back all the documents and her mobile. After taking the files he shot Sherly three times on her chest. Edwin was frightened and stood frozen. After ensuring her death, Colonel's men left. Hearing the noise of gun firing, Akshay ran to Sherly house. He saw a group of people getting into the car and fleeing the scene. Akshay entered the house and saw Edwin sitting and crying near the dead body of Sherly.

Akshay was sad and lost his temper for a minute. Sherly was like a sister to him. Akshay thought it was because of him Sherly got shot. Suddenly Akshay regained his mind. Akshay said its time to end that basted show forever. Now this is not just professional, now this is personal to me. He took his phone and called the police. The phone was ringing but nobody was taking the call. Akshay told Edwin I will go down the mountain and report everything to police. Akshay took his car and left home.

Ghost busted

Akshay started the car and went down the mountain road. After a while of driving, car started to showed some missing. Then engine has stopped. Akshay tried to start the engine again and again, but no use. He just got out of the car and looked around, nobody was nearby. It was not possible to go up the mountain with this dead car. He put the car in first gear and using brakes slowly slide down the car to bottom of the mountain. Now the car is going really slow like a cycle. Akshay was nerves when he reached near the danger hairpin bend road. There were no lights except cars head light. When he was at the U-shape bend of danger hairpin, suddenly a truck hit on the back of his car. The truck started to drag the car towards the edge of the mountain. Akshay suddenly opened the door and jumped out of the car. Without knowing this, truck driver dragged the car and thrown it off the mountain. Akshay managed to get on the back of the truck and silently moved towards the driver. He took a pistol and pointed towards the driver.

Akshay – "You are busted 'ghosty'. Hands up and place them where I can see."

The driver was wearing a black mask. Akshay asked the driver to get out of the truck slowly. But while out of truck, driver suddenly kicked the gun in Akshay's hand. Akshay lost the gun. Driver jumped on to Akshay and started a fight. Akshay retaliated with his full strength. Both of them got injured in the fight. Finally, Akshay managed to take down the driver. Using a rope in the car he tied the driver and made him stable. Akshay took off driver's mask and got surprised. It was Colonel's driver Joyal. With the gun pointed on to driver's head Akshay said

Akshay – "I am not a journalist, I am a Deputy Superintendent in CBI, working as an undercover agent for investigating this ghost truck case, don't even think I will hand over such a murderer like you to police alive. Now tell me everything, if you don't want to eat my bullet"

Driver – "Please don't kill me, I will tell you everything"

Driver started to spit the truth. Colonel is behind all these. All these killing, extortion everything is done by him. Colonel did all these to cover up his drug business. Whoever stands up as a threat to him and his business gets terminated.

Killer Truck / Ghost Truck

Secret of danger hairpin

Joyal started the story, he said Colonel and Joyal were together in Himachal base camp. Colonel and I relocated to this bungalow in Anandpur town for starting the drug business. Colonel gets drugs from mother ship coming from Afghan. Drug bags are collected by sending boats. But the bags of Drugs coming from the ship is not safe to store in his bungalow. Now Colonel wants a safe, hidden and invisible warehouse to store these drugs. He travelled Anandpur town for months in quest of such place. One day while travelling to down the mountain, he noticed a place near danger hairpin road. He decided to dig a huge hole in that place of mountain near danger hairpin to create an artificial cave. Colonel brought workers from distant states, so that no one will know about construction. These workers were accommodated in a house down the mountain, silently. In order to hide the construction, all works are carried out at night time. During the day time, mouth of the cave is covered by a huge carpet and a temporary wooden fruits selling booth is set up in front of the carpet. Everyone thought it was a new road side fruit seller and no one ever knew about the cave hole in the back of carpet. Colonel transported the workers and equipment's to construction area with the help of a truck driver named Jerome who lived in the Anandpur town. He told Jerome not to tell anyone about construction since they are going to make a tourist resort in this artificial cave which will be a surprise to town people and outside world, and must be disclosed only on the day of inauguration. Jerome kept the promise and told nothing to even his family and transported workers every day. But Colonel knew as the construction finishes, Jerome will disclose everything to town people. So on the last day of construction Colonel and his men, killed Jerome and all workers with gun. Jerome and check post guards were friends. If guards in the check post see someone else driving Jerome's truck they will notice it, so Colonel hide the truck inside the artificial cave. Now they removed all the camouflages used like carpet, wooden booth for fruit selling, etc. They closed the Cave mouth with huge rocks, now no one can find a cave in that place. Colonel kept all the drug bags in this cave warehouse and from there it is distributed to major cities like Bengaluru, Chennai and Kochi. At night Colonel's men removed one or two rocks in front of the cave for getting in and out and the cave warehouse. This cave is also used for all their mysterious activities and dirty works. But as time passes police and narcotics cell came to Anandpur to investigate about the source of drugs distributed from Mountain top. Colonel used the truck of Jerome, to create accidents to police vehicles thereby freezing all the investigation. After that truck is hidden in artificial cave. Then Colonel's men purposefully spread the story of Jerome's ghost creating these accidents, among the illiterate cattle farmers of Anandpur.

The trick of making accident is different as colonel is an evil genius. Colonel's men along with an expert car mechanic will reach the selected victims house at night. The car mechanic will damage the airbag system by cutting cables of airbag sensors. Now the airbag system will not work during an accident. After that Colonel's men shadow the victim for days. Accidents are created at night. When the victim comes towards the danger hairpin, Colonel's men pass the information to cave warehouse. The killer truck will be parked nearer to the danger hairpin hidden, on road side, behind trees, covering with a black cloth, no one can spot the truck in that darkness. When the victim reaches the U-shape bend of the hairpin, truck suddenly hits on the back of victim's car. Drag the car to edge of mountain and throw it off. Every light in the hairpin area would be destroyed by Colonel's men on morning itself. Truck would be coming with its head light off to hit victim's car. So in that dark night, victim can only see the truck when it hits on the back of victim's car. This creates an illusion, that a truck suddenly appeared like a magic and hit on the back of the car. The truck was then hidden in the cave. The injuries and damages in victim's body and victim's car would exactly look like a normal accident. Since death of victim is by fall of car from mountain, no scientific investigation can find anything abnormal. In Both forensic report and postmortem report everything will be just like a normal accident. There would be no clues or scientific evidence to prove it as a planned accident. The victim's car is falling down to mountain trench of a depth 100 feet, without airbag system. There is a ninety nine percent chance of victim's death.

Many of the police officers were killed that way, also some of the natives who had doubts on colonel's business. Veterinary doctor coming to visit cattle farms in town from down the mountain once felt some doubts about Colonel's mysterious business and the helicopter visiting Colonel's bungalow. He started to fetch his curiosity by enquiring more information. He was killed next day in an accident. Many of the natives who enquires more about Colonel's business were also killed in accidents along with some innocent people, this is to balance the death database sheet or else outside world will think, they were manipulated accidents.

Colonel ran his drug cartel smoothly like this manner. But soon police started their investigation about these accidents. They started to fix CCTV cameras at danger hairpin and other hidden cameras nearby. This really choked Colonel's drug business. Because of cameras, making accidents became impossible. Also getting in and out of the cave became very difficult. Colonel was in deep thought for finding a way out of this crisis. Suddenly something came up in his mind and he smiled like a winner. Colonel went up-stairs of his bungalow and started to search something. He came up with a brief case and there was a hard disk in it, which contains a miracle. When colonel was in army, on deputation he was posted to Defence Research and Development Organization (DRDO) for some time. DRDO was developing many new weapons and devices for Indian Army. They kept all the data of their research in the main frame computer. Colonel copied many of these data's to a hard disk, his intention was to sell this data to enemy countries and make money. Electromagnetic Pulse Gun (EMP gun) was a device made by DRDO for Indian army. This gun will produce Electromagnetic pulse wave in three kilometer radius which will destroy the electronic circuits in its range. EMP gun will overload every electronic circuit in its range and thus destroys the circuits. This was made for Indian army to use in the chicken neck of Chinese border for destroying Chinese electronic devices and communication facilities. The data regarding EMP gun was also in Colonels hard disk. The data includes full step to create and use this EMP gun. Colonel hired some scientists who were specialized in electronics and in no time, he made the EMP gun and hidden it in artificial cave warehouse. From there he operated the EMP gun and produced electromagnetic pulse waves which destroyed CCTV's, hidden cameras, mobiles and every electronic devices in three kilometer radius. Thus Colonel managed to solve that problem and continued his business.

Then police went up with new strategy of posting police constables at danger turn for guarding. Colonel was a coldblooded murder and for him it was not a difficult task to kidnap and kill poor police men. Thus police absolutely surrendered before the ghost truck case and intentionally ignored Anandpur town and its people.

Artificial cave warehouse built by Colonel in the mountain

EMP Gun (Electromagnetic Pulse Weapons)

Helicopter for smuggling

Zameer Ali's Boss will send Drug bags in large container ships. The ship will anchor in outer sea. Drug lord's like, Colonel and others will send boats to collect their share of drug bags from ship. This is then shifted to their own warehouse's and from there distributed to cities like Bengaluru, Chennai, etc. for further small-scale distribution. But as time passes government become more vigilant and strong actions were taken against drug cartel operations. Navy and coast guard are conducting strong patrol in sea. Many of the drug paddlers boats are captured and busted. Transfer of drugs from boats to warehouse was also Risky. Police and Narcotics squad were really vigilant and many of the consignments were captured. But retail value of party drugs like MDMA and meth in cities are 200 times than the whole sale value from mother ships. Thus no one was ready to abandoned this business. Every time when a drug bust occurs only hatchet men gets arrested and prosecuted. Drug loads will hire new hatchet men and continue their business. Drug loads have no commitments towards their hatchet men. They will only know that when they get captured by police. When a drug consignment gets caught, crores of money is lost and also information about warehouse, identities of drug lord's and many other things are at risk, so busting is still a head ache.

Colonel's Airbus Helicopter for smuggling

Here our Colonel was thinking one step ahead of others. Colonel already earned a large amount of profit from this business. Money was not a big deal for Colonel. So he bought an Airbus helicopter to reinforce his drug business. When in Himachal base camp Colonel had a friend called Peter who was a tourist, sight-seeing helicopter pilot. Both were bar mates and drunkard. When Colonel invited, Peter joined us without any hesitation.

With the help of Peter Colonel started smuggling of drugs in helicopter. Peter will take the helicopter to mothership. Without landing, helicopter will stand still, twenty feet above the ship. A rope is put down to ship from helicopter. Drug bags are tied to this rope and Colonel's men in helicopter will pull up the rope and collect the drug bags. Similarly, during the night when everyone is at sleep, helicopter reaches near the Colonel's bungalow. In the backyard of Colonel's bungalow there are three red beacon lights fixed on trees on upward direction. This is for signaling the helicopter. This three lights form a V-shape which is a land mark for the helicopter to drop the package, which are drug bags. Here also helicopter will not land and stand still 30 feet above ground and drop the package and leave.

Our police force and narcotics cell don't have helicopters for transportation and investigation. So Colonel continued his drug smuggling easily without any threat. Police don't even have a clue about Colonel and his smuggling through sky, they were busy with other drug lords who do smuggling by boats and cars. But many of the drug lords were jealous about Colonel, they gave information about Colonel's smuggling to police. Thus many police officers came to Anandpur for investigating against Colonel. They were all killed in made up accidents in danger hairpin bend road. Thus every investigation were frozen by Colonel.

Anandpur people have no idea why this helicopter is passing this many times across the mountain. Some of the people reported seeing the helicopter circling near Colonel's bungalow. Colonel denied everything and always explained these as rumors spread by his enemies for destroying his good will in the society.

Truck driver whispered "this is all I know, colonel is behind everything, I am ready to tell all these truth before any court. Please don't hurt me again."

Akshy patiently heard everything the driver said, just like child hearing a story. After that he fell into a deep thought process, rewound every incident in mind. Now every chain is connected, everything is crystal clear. It is the time to dash. He suddenly stood up, took the ghost truck along with driver to the police superintendent's office. Considering the serious situation police superintendent reached the office in no time, even if it was late night. Akshy uncovered that he is an undercover CBI officer and presented the ghost truck and driver. Akshay explained everything about Colonel and cave warehouse and convinced the truth of danger hairpin accidents to police superintendent. Akshay also contacted CBI headquarters and reported everything. Akshay requested CBI director to arrange some CRPF force from nearby state camps to help them. Police superintendent ordered his police force to get ready for an operation. Every police-men reported and got ready with arms and ammunitions. Police force along with Akshay started from police headquarters prepared for a fire fight. They are going to raid the warehouse at night itself. They reached the danger hairpin and spotted the artificial cave as told by Joyal. Using dynamites, they blasted rocks in cave mouth. There were tons of drugs stored in that warehouse. Since it was a surprise attack there were only 15 of Colonel's men, but still they are armed with modern machine guns, grenades, etc. There were shooting from both sides. Lots of men get injured and killed in this, on both sides. But police were large in numbers and outwitted the villains. All the bad guys were killed, except one or two, they just surrendered to police. Police took all the drug bags, equipment's, EMP gun, files from the cave and arrested the Colonel's men and took everything to police headquarters in down town. It took the whole night to complete the process. On early morning Akshay and police superintendent took the ghost truck driver to Judicial first class Majistrate and explained everything. Majistrate issued a warrant against Colonel.

At morning six trucks of CRPF soldiers armed with machine-guns arrived from CRPF camps of nearby states as directed by central government. Police superintendent also gave Akshay a battalion of armed force for arresting colonel. Superintendent wished him luck and advised him be careful and catch that monster dead or alive. Don't hesitate to use bullets at will and this must be the last sunrise of that basted. Akshay along with police and CRPF started from there, ready to fight a small war.

The end game

Colonel's men and Akshay's men

Knowing the information about his arrest, Colonel called for his helicopter to escape. Also he called all of his remaining men to resist the police. Nearly sixty of Colonels men gathered at Colonel's bungalow with most modern machine guns, grenades, RPG's, rocket launchers, etc. which were smuggled from Pakistan. Akshay and his men took their position in front of Colonel's bungalow with arms. Akshay announced through the loud speaker for villains to surrender but Colonel's men started firing. A huge fire exchange occurred between both sides. Meanwhile inside, Colonel was packing his solid cash currency in bags. The fight between hero's and villains continued for half an hour.

Helicopter arrived in no time, it doesn't land, but stood just 20 feet above the bungalows roof. Colonel suddenly appeared in the bungalows roof with four huge bags of solid cash, he asked to put down the rope from helicopter. He tied the money bags on the rope and told his men in helicopter to pull up the money bags. After that his men put down a rope ladder from the helicopter, for the Colonel to climb. Colonel started climbing the ladder. When reached the middle of ladder, he heard a gun-shot. Colonel looked back, he saw Akshay and some police men standing on the roof pointing gun towards him and helicopter. Akshay warned colonel.

Akshay : "surrender , else we will be forced to fire at will"

Colonel stood still for a moment thinking. But suddenly he restarted climbing without looking back. Aksay decided to give a final warning by firing gun two times, to the sky. But hearing this random gun shots pilot thought police started firing towards pilot and helicopter. If a bullet hits on the fuel tank of helicopter everything will explode. Since pilot is just a normal homosapien, who loves and values his own life more than anything, he took the helicopter forward with full speed, ignoring his boss and money bags. Colonel was at the middle of rope ladder, when helicopter started moving, he stopped climbing and hold the ladder tight. Colonel managed to hold the rope for some time but due to harsh and fast movement of helicopter, his hands slipped from the rope ladder. Colonel fell before the cops on the ground in bungalow's front and died. The money bags also fell from the helicopter which hit on the sides of helicopter and branches of the trees down and got open causing a rain of currency notes on the ground. Colonel got the taste of same death, that he gave to his victims, falling from heights. On the impact of fall, Colonel's veins were bursts just like a water balloon, blood flown out of his dead body just like water leaking from a pipe. Colonel's body was on the ground upside down in the middle of a pool of blood. Akshy approached the body on the ground and flipped the head and watched Colonel's opened eyes and terrifying face. Currency notes were all over the dead body and around it. Akshay slowly stood up, put his pistol back to its cover. Akshay murmured to a police constable nearby.

Akshay : "After all these killing, extortion, crimes, drug trafficking and burning the youth, he can't carry a penny to his way to hell except his bag of sins earned during a life time. No one is born as a criminal but in the life's race he is ready to do anything for money. Colonel's picture will be all over the media tomorrow, would it become a lesson to everyone. No, after few days, public will remember nothing and will be back with what they were doing. Everyone is deliberately forgetting the basic fact that we are all born just to die ...... just to die...... "

Sun set was as normal as everyday. Night flashed its dark cloth above the Colonel's bungalow and Anandpur town, but this time it was different, every mystery untied, every bit of fear erased, town people enjoyed that extreme calmness and exchanged their curiosities about the events and freedomful, fearless future.

As Akshay said Colonel's news were all over the media and discussed for few days after that people got back to their own business as nothing happened, so do Akshay, enjoying in the first class seat of Etihad Airways, Boeing 777x aircraft, on his way back to CBI headquarters in CGO complex at New Delhi, with his eyes closed, enjoying the music through headphone, until the day another colonel comes up with another new mystery.

Boeing 777x Aircraft

Some facts and real events

News Headings - 1 (May 14, 2023) – India's biggest drug bust in history: Narcotics and Navy seized methamphetamine worth Rs. 15,000 crores from Indian Waters near Kochi, Pakistani citizen arrested

Kochi : The Narcotics Control Bureau(NCB) and Indian Navy seized around 2,500 kg of methamphetamine from Indian waters off Kochi. The seized drugs are worth around Rs. 15,000 crores in the market and, according to NCB officials, amount to the largest seizure by any Indian enforcement agency in terms of value. 134 sacks of methamphetamine were recovered from ship. A Pakistani national was arrested.

Pictures of drugs captured from boat and a Pakistani citizen seized

NCB officer said "we have been carrying out operation 'Samudragupt' to make Indian waters drug-free as per directions from government. We got inputs regarding a mother ship carrying methamphetamine passing through Indian waters. We intercepted it with the support of Indian Navy. The mother vessel couldn't be seized as it sank. We have arrested a Pakistan national in connection with this case. The vessels are originating from the Chabahar coast, were laden with methamphetamine made in Pakistan. The consignment was intended for sale in India, Sri Lanka and Maldives. These drugs are coming from Iran, Pakistan and Afghanistan."

This is also the first interception of a mother ship carrying drugs by an Indian agency. The seizure is a part of Operation 'Samudragupt' targeting maritime trafficking of drugs aimed at making the Indian Ocean region free of narcotics. The operation has been initiated by inputs from sources developed by the Navy Intelligence and the NCB. An Indian Navy ship was deployed in the region leading to the interception of the ship.

The modus operandi is to halt the mother ship at a particular point at which the crew in the ship receives a message about the boat to which the drug is to be offloaded and its timing. Since, the mother ship itself has been intercepted, there is no information on any boat or person supposed to take delivery of it.

News Headings – 2 (Oct 31, 2022) : Pakistan Using China made Drones to smuggle weapons, explosives and drugs in Kashmir.

Srinagar : Pakistan has now started a new game of smuggling weapons and narcotics through drones. Nefarious designs of Pakistan are not hidden. They are now smuggling weapons, narcotics and improved explosive devices (IED). Pakistan is continuously trying to disturb the peace in J & K but mechanism to counter Pakistan is strong. Villagers in the border area reported sighting a suspected drone-type object near the International Border, following which the police carried out a search operation. In the face of increased drone activity and the smuggling of weapons and narcotics, Punjab is helping J & K in dealing with the rouge drone menace.

Pakistan has made consistent efforts to smuggle arms and ammunition through drones to indulge in some major terror attacks. In June 2021, two drones carrying explosives were used in a terrorist attack on an Indian Air Force base. The use of drones for arm drops poses a serious threat to national security, as it allows terrorists to bypass traditional border security measures and infiltrate the country. It is a challenging task to detect them and their ability to fly at low altitudes, making them difficult to detect by radar. The government has taken several steps to address the issue, including the establishment of anti-drone systems and the use of technology to detect and intercept drones. The Army and other security agencies are also using advanced technology, such as sensors and cameras, to monitor and track the movement of drones along the border. Overall, the use of drones for arm drops is a serious security concern, and the government needs to continue to invest in technology and infrastructure to prevent such incidents from happening in the future. The terrorist groups and ISI are using the upgraded version of drone which is bigger and can carry large quantities of firearms. Pakistan through its agencies and different terror factions is dropping weapons through drones in Punjab, which is meant to terrorist activities in J & K.

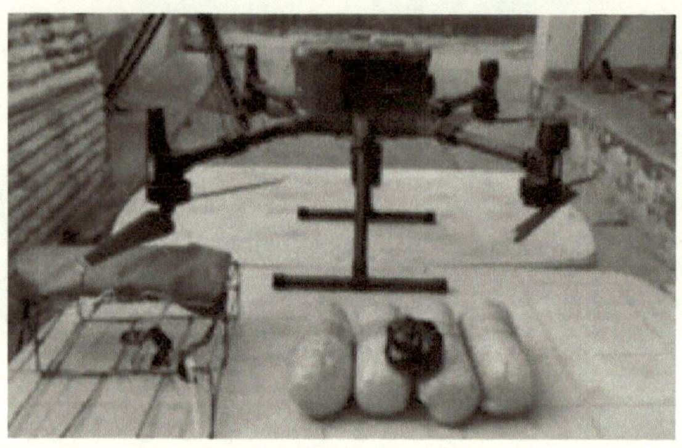

Pakistan drones caught by army

Electromagnetic Pulse Gun or Electromagnetic Pulse weapons

Electromagnetic pulse gun (EMP gun) is an electronic device with an antenna, which produces electromagnetic pulse waves. These electromagnetic pulse waves overload's every electronic circuit in its radius range. Thus every electronic equipment in its range are destroyed. These emp waves are also produced during a nuclear explosion. Many countries like USA, China, Russia are already having lots EMP weapons. These are mainly used to destroy enemy communication systems during a war. Many countries developed emp bombs for using in warfare. This

emp waves are non-lethal.

Huge EMP Gun for USA Military with larger range of destruction capacity
(Electromagnetic Pulse Weapons)

Air Bag System in Cars

Airbag system contains a collision sensor which gets activated while accident occurs. This sensor sends an electric signal to produce nitrogen gas inside air bags by a small chemical reaction, during an accident. This nitrogen gas gets filled in air bags of car and save the victim during an accident. If the wires to sensors are cut, then sensor will not send a signal to produce nitrogen gas which fills the air bag. Thus air bags will not work, if the connection to sensors are cut.

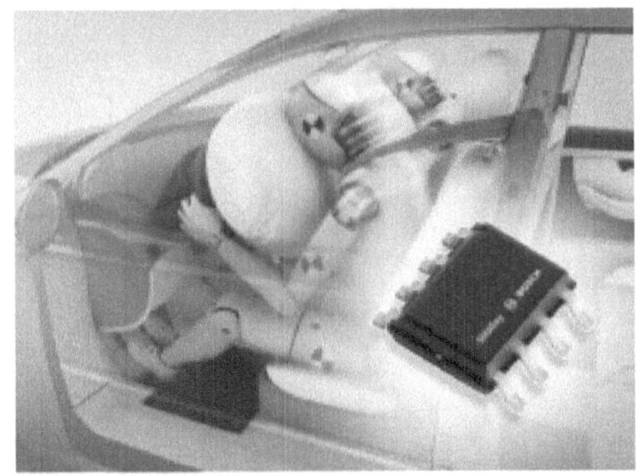

Airbag system and collision sensor

S – 400 Triumph

S 400 is a mobile surface-to-air missile (SAM) system developed in 1990s by Russia. India signed a USD 5.5 billion deal with Russia in Oct 2018 to acquire five S – 400 systems for IAF. Russia delivered the first two systems to India in December 2021 and April 2022. Two other systems will be delivered by the end of 2023. The first S 400 system is deployed in India's northwest Punjab region to mitigate air threats from China and Pakistan. The second system is deployed in the northeast region of the country. The third will be deployed in the western Rajasthan region along Pakistan. According to experts Russia's S 400 is more efficient than America's missile defence system 'Thad'. In Thad, missiles can only be sent in one direction. For changing direction, the device has to be moved left or right. But in S 400 system the missiles are send in upward direction after that the missile will automatically change its direction as ordered.

S 400 System

Drugs like Methamphetamine and MDMA
Methamphetamine

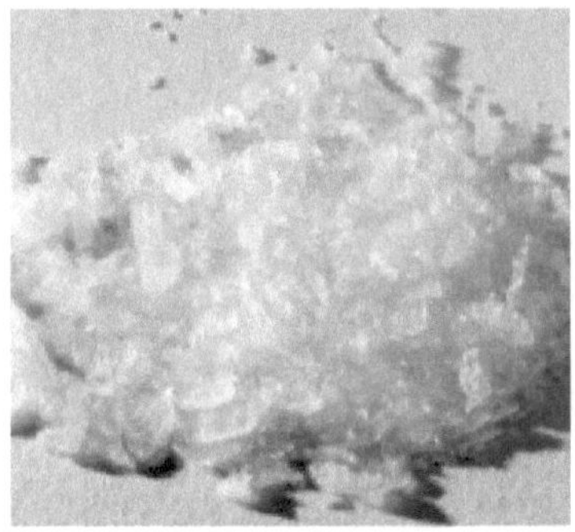

Methamphetamine

It is a psycho stimulant drug which is also called as meth, crystal meth, shabu, etc. Its bad effects in humans are Attention-deficit hyperactivity disorder (ADHD), Obesity and Narcolepsy (sleep disorder). Mostly meth is produced from Pseudoephedrine. It can be seen as tablets, bluish white crystals and powder. It can be consumed by Swallowing, smoking and injecting. Meth increases the neuro transmitter in brain called as dopamine. Short term effect of meth are Brain elevation mood and alertness, Increased heart rate, Increased breath rate, promotes weight loss. Long term effect of meth are extreme weight loss, severe dental damage, Anxiety, sleeping disorder, violent behaviors. Overdose of meth causes psychosis, heart attacks, seizures, strokes, organ failures and even death.

MDMA

MDMA is a party drug also known as ecstasy, molly, etc. It is a stimulant drug chemically related to amphetamine. It causes increased alertness and positive mood. It also causes unique prosocial effects like reduced social inhibition, increased sociability, strong feeling of trust, openness and closeness, etc. By inhibiting transporter proteins, MDMA causes serotonin, dopamine and norepinephrine to accumulate in synaptic cleft and increases neurotransmitter activity there. MDMA is scientifically known as 3,4-methylenedioxy-N-methylamphetamine. MDMA releases lots of neurotransmitters called serotonin in brain which causes happiness and good mood. But when the patient comes out of the drug, there will deficit of serotonin in brain which causes bad mood, tiredness, anxiety, etc.

MDMA

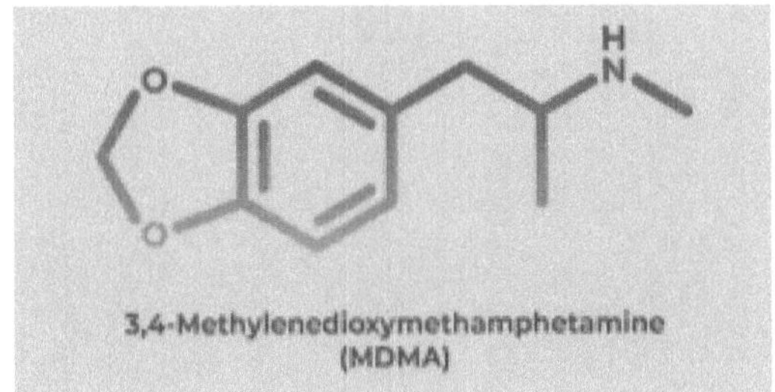

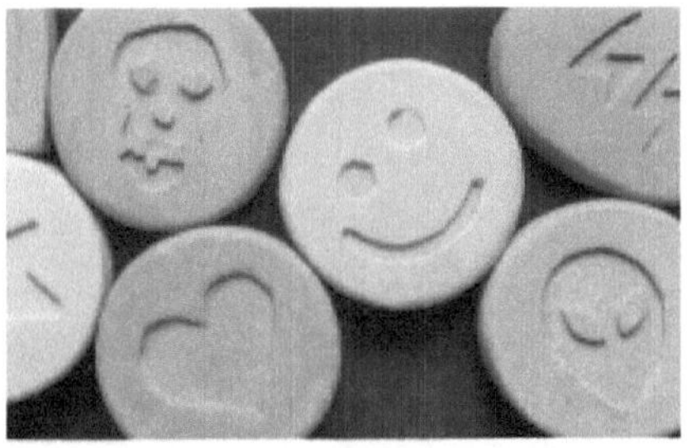

Author's Name – Thapandas E Menon
Story Type – Detective, Thriller, Fiction
Story Source – Author's Imagination